It is advisable therefore to amuse yourselves before you introduce your member and accomplish the act. You will excite her by kissing her cheeks, sucking her lips, and nibbling her teats. You will kiss her navel and thighs, and lay a provoking hand upon her pubes. Bite her arms; do not neglect any part of her body; clasp her tightly till she feels your love; then sigh and twine your arms and legs around hers.

The Perfumed Garden
Sheikh Nefzawi
1886 translation by Sir Richard Burton

33/50

Picasso

THE CLITORAL KISS

A Fun Guide to
Oral Sex,
Oral Massage,
and Other Oral Delights

by

Kenneth Ray Stubbs, Ph.D.

with

Chyrelle D. Chasen

Illustrated
by
Kyle Spencer
Deborah Harvey
David Thorpe, Richard Stodart
Pablo Picasso, Betty Dodson, Rick van Genderen, Mario Tauzin

Secret Garden
Larkspur, CA

Published by   Secret Garden
                      P.O. Box 67- KCA
                      Larkspur, California 94977– 0067
Copyright © 1993 by Kenneth Ray Stubbs, Ph.D.
All rights reserved.   Printed in the United States of America.
Illustrations: Kyle Spencer, Deborah Harvey, David Thorpe, Richard
                   Stodart, Betty Dodson, Pablo Picasso, Mario Tauzin
Book Design: Deborah Harvey
Cover Photo: David Thorpe
Author's Photo: Jim Dennis
ISBN 0-939263-08-4

Also by Kenneth Ray Stubbs, Ph.D.
        Romantic Interludes: A Sensuous Lovers Guide
        Erotic Massage: The Touch of Love
        Sacred Orgasms: Teachings from the Heart

ROMANTIC
INTERLUDES
A Sensuous Lovers Guide
Kenneth Ray Stubbs, Ph.D. with Louise-Andrée Saulnier
Foreword by Beverly Whipple, Ph.D., co-author, *The G Spot*

Dedicated to
Special Lips

Evelyn
Sherry
Cassy
Louise

Acknowledgments

Chyrelle D. Chasen, my friend and collaborator, is the catalyst behind this book. Her gentle persuasion keeps me on target.

Sandy Trupp, my friend and publishing advisor, is a continuous inspiration.

Deborah Harvey, the book's designer, has a wonderfully creative right brain.

Kyle Spencer, one of the principal illustrators, brings a soft sensuality to the oral expression.

Richard Stodart's paintings and David Thorpe's photography bring, respectively, a reverent and playful aura to oral passion.

Vicki Folz patiently transcribed my words while providing insightful feedback.

Karen Kummerfeldt was a great help in Talk Dirty To Me.

The owners, salespeople, and customers of Serendipity and Loveseason provided much of the colorful, provocative terminology.

Many thanks to Harley SwiftDeer Reagan, president and founder of The Rainbow Powers Educational and Healing Center, for permission to use the "Sex Shake" formula.

I greatly appreciate the National Gay and Lesbian Task Force for the up-to-date information on the legal status of oral sex in the U.S.

Many others assisted in many ways: Carole Merette, Carolyn Parker, Chris Folz, Chris McMahon, Clara Kerns, Corinna Kavanagh, Dolores Bishop, Evelyn Barnes, Jennifer Lively, Jennifer Whitaker, Pam Johnson, Sandy McCune, Saunya Tolson, Tahara Allen.

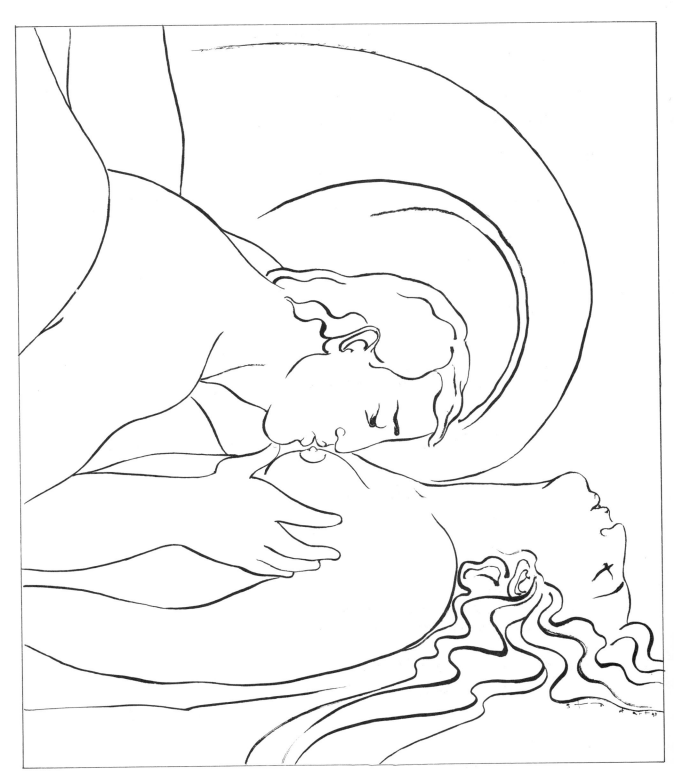

Richard Stodart

Table of Contents

DISCLAIMER

The author, illustrator, and publisher shall have neither liability nor responsibility to any person or entity with respect to any loss, damage, injury, or ailment caused or alleged to be caused directly or indirectly by the information or lack of information in this book.

Some of the techniques in this book would be considered "unsafe sexual practices" if either partner is infected with any transmittable disease. Please consult a physician or health practitioner.

Section I:

A

PERSONAL

INTRODUCTION

KYLE SPENCER

KISS & TELL — AN ORAL AUTOBIOGRAPHY

Oral lovemaking is about more than techniques. It is about the human experience. This is my personal story of how I discovered my oral sexuality.

Evelyn and I were high school sweethearts. These were pre-pill, teen years, a time when *good* girls *didn't*. What we did do was kissing, lips to lips, and necking. Fragrances of Old Spice and Shalimar lace memories of humid summer evenings while we parked in my mother's car, a green '53 Ford Club Coupe, in Bryan Park.

I wanted to go all the way. She probably did too. But the puritanical mores and the fear of pregnancy kept us kissing—for hours and hours. Kissing for hours, slow dancing to Johnny Mathis, "It's heavenly, heavenly/each time our lips touch/breathlessly." Kissing for hours, on our first date, a water-skiing trip down on the river. I could feel the sun burning my back the whole afternoon. I didn't care. Evelyn's lips were full, moist with red lipstick, more like Marilyn Monroe's smiling invitation than Brigitte Bardot's erotic pout.

At thirteen while hormones ush-ered in new urges, the basic skills of kissing began. I started playing the trumpet. The secret is in the embou-chure, holding the lips tightly together while forced air from the diaphragm vibrates the lip membranes. Add the ta ta ta ta, the ta-ca ta-ca, and the ta-de-ca ta-de-ca of the tongue and you have the agility and endurance for hours of kiss-ing. Evelyn always smiled when she said her lips were tired.

Before the trumpet, before Evelyn, was Spin the Bottle and other games. My first erotic kiss came at about nine, playing Hide and Seek. Somehow a girl and I ended up in the same dark closet. One thing led to another. That kiss, and it was only a kiss, elicited a new, strange, swelling sensation in my pelvis. It was wonderful and I didn't know why or what.

Not for another eleven hormone-wacky years, until I was twenty, would I have what we think of as "the real thing": sexual intercourse. In the mean-while, I participated in the age-old ritual known as *frottage*. Fully clothed, my date and I would rub our chests, abdomens, pelvises, and thighs together, almost to the point of friction burns. Always accompanying was a fiery passion play of only lips and tongues probing, thrusting, circling, sucking, tasting. This ritual insured virginity and prevented pregnancy, was frantically frustrating, but better than nothing.

When I finally went *all the way*, it was disappointing. All the years of hoping, fantasizing, and making out, had set high expectations. Disappointment, however, didn't deter from trying again. Hormone-driven desires, like tornadoes, find few obstacles.

Then I met Shannon. By now I was teaching sociology in a small northeastern college. The Beatles had progressed from *I Want to Hold Your Hand* to *Why Don't We Do It in the Road*. Bob Dylan was shifting from the social protest of *Blowin' in the Wind* to lyrics about liberated women, "She's an artist/She don't look back."

The first evening we met, Shannon invited me to go to bed. Finally fantasy emerged as reality: the woman was the sexual initiator. In a daze, I could barely stutter out, "But I don't know you." Two hours later I recanted. Twenty-four hours later, without any disappointments, I waddled home, bowlegged and sore and very sexually satisfied. It was the beginning of three years of loving, kissing, cuddling, licking, sucking, and balling, the popular, descriptive term of the day. Fully-clothed frottage was now a part of the play, no longer a Victorian substitute. All across the country, traveling in our VW van, at any frequent flare of passion, we would pull over, close the drapes, and proclaim the bumper sticker slogan, "If this van is rockin', don't bother knockin'."

The love and the sex were good to the very end. But we had evolved in different directions, and it was time to follow separate paths. Shannon went back East to become a poet. I headed off to Mexico to study Spanish.

There in the mystical mountains of this land of immense beauty, I went through love withdrawal. I felt terribly alone. I missed the sex but I missed more the contact, the holding, the cuddling. The full sexual awakening with Shannon had really been an awakening to the basic human need of touch.

Where next? Academia lacked soul for me now; the ivory tower was no longer an ascension to meaningful knowledge. So I chose North to San Francisco, the counter-culture mecca.

Masters degrees in Sociology were a dime-a-dozen in San Francisco in

1973. The first job I found was selling tickets part-time at the Saturday-night underground midnight movies. The rest of the week this converted mainstream cinema played porn flicks. Large screen images of breasts, penises, buttocks, and wet labia with stereo moaning, groaning, and orgasmic peaks were both shocking and titillating—but only for a few weeks. Fucking and sucking, sucking and fucking day in and day out became unbearably boring.

Then *Deep Throat* was busted in New York. This humorous, grade-D flick, starring Linda "The Devil Made Me Do It" Lovelace and Harry Reems, received so much notoriety that Middle America flocked to see Linda *give head* to Harry in a way many never thought possible. She swallowed the whole thing, really! The fantasy part of the plot was, "Doctor, the tingle's not down there. It's in my throat." Obviously the doctor has to give an authentic examination, and by George, Linda's clitoris really is in her throat.

Viewers—couples, single men, single women, senior citizens—were walking out of the sold-out, 800-seat theater with new visions and new fantasies. Oral sex had moved from underneath the covers out into the public domain.

Deep Throat had a different meaning for me. From all the extra working hours, I finally had enough finances to go to massage school. It wouldn't be Shannon's touch, but it would be lots of touch.

Massage school was great. Not only did I practice all the new strokes, I got to receive them. For hours and hours it was each student's duty to lie back and receive. My aching neck, my weary brow, my sore back, they were in heaven. Except for one little, nagging concern: What if I get an erection?

Sooner or later massage therapists have to come to terms with the issue of sexual feelings. In a professional massage it's okay for the "client" to cry if sad, pound pillows if anger comes up, but don't get *turned on*. Massage school teaches a donut massage—there's a hole in the middle. *Down There*, the genital area, is off limits.

After a couple of years of doing professional massage and teaching numerous massage seminars, I decided to break with tradition. More important than the specific massage techniques, I had discovered, the essence of massage is really the presence, the sensitivity, the awareness. Why not teach couples how to give loving, nurturing touch to all the body, including the genitals? This was the birth of my Erotic Massage for Couples seminar.

But how do you teach something you don't know? It became a time of "You show me yours, I'll show you mine." The adult version of "Playing Doctor" is a lot more fun.

I felt sort of like a Columbus sailing off into uncharted waters. Would the seminar get out of hand and turn into an orgy? Would one partner in a couple make a pass at another? Would everybody just freak out and leave? Fortunately, my fears were unfounded. We didn't sail off the deep end. Eventually this seminar was to become a training program for sex therapists and the basis of my book and video, *Erotic Massage — The Touch of Love.*

What about *advanced* erotic massage? Many couples had found their first seminar to be a romantic Bed and Breakfast weekend with instructions — a sort of second honeymoon away from kids, phone calls, and grocery shopping. In the first weekend I had followed the underlying principles theorized by Masters and Johnson: non-performance and non-demand. Let go of trying to prove you're the best lover in town, let go of expectations, and like a mountain stream, flow with the un-

folding feelings of the moment, erotic and otherwise. Now in the advanced course, following the same philosophy, I introduced oral techniques, a massage using the lips, the tongue, the teeth, and the breath.

Biting on grapes to get more saliva flowing, we started with the Ice Cream Lick on the forearms. Then came the Suck, Slide, and Twirl up and down the inner arm. Some practiced The Lollipop stroke on fingers and toes. You might hear a few giggles by now. Next maybe The Clitoral Kiss stroke on earlobes. A few more teehees. By the time we came to The Motorboat on the abdomen, the whole room was laughing and squirming. Couples were like kids again.

A few years later I was invited to a conference in Colorado to give a presentation. The topic: Sexuality and Professional Massage. It was a warm spring day with fresh breezes from the nearby Rockies as the female cab driver pulled up in front of my hotel. Urban cowgirl fantasies flashed through my mind.

"What brings you to Denver?" she inquired, her eyes smiling into the rearview mirror. I figured I had nothing to lose revealing the intimate details. "Oh, I do massage too," she chuckled. A few more flirting exchanges and she accepted my invitation to a Tiger Love Bite on her neck. I would never advise such potent erotic play while driving down the freeway but this was one of those moments when you cast doubts to the wind. Gently I sank my teeth into her trapezius muscle.

"I could just turn the meter off and pull over for a while," I heard her say as I released the bite. How do you turn down a once-in-a-lifetime offer when you're running late? This time I had to decline. Yet it felt complete and satisfying, for each of us I think, as a dance of fantasies sealed with a kiss. "Almost" was more exciting than "all the way."

Apparently there weren't (and still aren't) many people publicly teaching about oral lovemaking when an editor of a national magazine invited me to write an article. "The Tasty Art of Oral Massage" was a simple, how-to set of instructions, a sensual guide to oral sex. When I handed out reprints in one of my training programs, a nurse asked permission to give copies to some of her spinal cord injury patients. When the sensation and the use of your genitals and hands are completely or severely limited, how do you make love?

How do you express, how do you consummate your sexual desire?

Ironically, I had just written my own lover's manual. Ten years later a neck injury was to leave me in a quadriplegic condition, paralyzed completely almost from my shoulders down to my toes. My genitals had been the main area of sexual pleasure, my hands the main way I expressed love and sexual desire. Now with only some sensations and physical functioning slowly returning in those areas, my lips, tongue, teeth and breath have become my principle means of play and passion.

I have written *The Clitoral Kiss* with all people in mind. Whether our emotions are erotic or not, our physical body fully functional or not, we are all sexual in nature. How we choose to express this nature is uniquely individual. My hope is that you will find the words in this book to be informative, stimulating, and liberating.

Except for the "Ancient Love Manuals" appendix, all of the following techniques have come out of my personal experience. They are a part of the dance of romance, the touch of love.

Section II:

THE TECHNIQUES

INVITATION

"FEVER WHEN YOU KISS ME." "SEALED WITH A KISS." "SMOTHER [your lover] IN CHOCOLATE SYRUP AND BOOGIE TILL THE COWS COME HOME." THE KISS, AS REPRESENTED IN OUR POPULAR LYRICS, IS SENSUAL, SEXUAL, PASSIONATE, AND ROMANTIC.

OUR FIRST DATE, OUR FIRST LOVE, OUR FIRST SEX ARE OFTEN SEALED WITH A KISS DEEP IN OUR MEMORIES. THE LIPS, THE TONGUE, THE TEETH, THE BREATH ARE AN INTEGRAL FACET OF MOST INTIMATE MOMENTS.

The Clitoral Kiss IS A GUIDE INTO THE SENSUAL REALM OF ORAL LOVEMAKING. THE TASTES, THE SMELLS, THE TOUCHES, EVEN THE SOUNDS ARE A PART OF AN EROTIC ART BOTH PRIMAL AND SOPHISTI-CATED, INTENSELY SERIOUS YET SPONTANEOUSLY PLAYFUL.

I INVITE YOU AND YOUR LOVER TO SHARE YOUR BODY, MIND, AND HEART IN A BASIC HUMAN EXPRESSION: THE KISS, CLITORAL OR ANYWHERE ELSE YOU SO DESIRE.

TDTM: Talk Dirty to Me

No one I know makes love in Latin, "cunnilingus" (oral sex on female genitals) or "fellatio" (oral sex on male genitals), except in text books. Most of us are far more expressive, far more colorful.

Here is what we usually say:

- Eating at the Y
- Nob Job
- Mustache Ride
- Playing the Flute
- Licking the Lollipop
- Going Down
- Eating Out
- Blowing the One-Eyed Boa
- Suck Job
- Lick Me
- Eat Pussy
- Suck Cock
- Deep Throat
- Muff Diving
- Suck Start a Harley
- Boxed Lunch
- Clit Nibble
- The Hoover
- Sit on My Face
- Eat Me
- Blow Job
- Eating Cherry Pie
- Tu Kan Chew
- 69
- Tube Steak
- Give Head
- Fur Burger with Side of Thighs
- Weenie Workout
- Suck the Chrome Off a Trailer Hitch

Why Don't We Do It In The Road

OR ANYWHERE WE WANT. UNDER THE COVERS, in the bed, with THE LIGHTS OUT is fine. WHEN WE WANT MORE spice, HERE ARE A few other locations we might try. (IN public places be discreet.)

- IN department store dressing stalls
- IN A CANOE
- While he's driving the car
  especially in a traffic jam
- While she's driving the car
  accomplishable only if you have a long tongue or if
  there's lots of room between the steering wheel and
  the thighs.
- IN the office after everyone else has gone home
- IN the back row of a movie theater
  (or the back pew of an uncrowded church)
- While hanging from a trapeze
  (seriously, but close to the ground)
- IN a phone booth

- Underwater in a swimming pool
- Riding in a rent-a-limo
- On a picnic table in the park
- On night flights under a blanket
- On any flight, sitting on the basin in those compact compartments
- On the handle bars of a motorcycle
- In a large oak tree, hanging on tightly
- While stuck on the top of a Ferris wheel
- In a restaurant underneath the table cloth
- In a chair lift
- A real quickie: In the elevator

YOUR POSITION OR MINE?

Sit
Stand
Lie
Kneel
Female on top
Male on top
This degree
That degree
This angle
That angle

More important than the position is the approach, the
   attitude:
1. Are you comfortable?
2. Are you willing to experiment?
3. Are you willing to play?

"69" is the most notorious oral sex position, of course. Here is something better.

- Start with two heavy duty eyebolts firmly secured in the ceiling. Attached are two sets of straps connected to a cloth seat. In this commercially available "love swing" your lover reclines with knees elevated and thighs spread. Park yourself in a comfortable chair and enter a feast for hours. Neck aches are rare the next morning.

Top Secrets

We can be a technician with 1001 techniques or a masterful artist. Here are some of my basics for the art of oral lovemaking.

1. Suction, Suction, Suction.

With most kisses, with many nibbles and bites, with most tongue strokes, use suction. Sometimes gently, sometimes intensely. The suction, it feels like, brings the nerve endings to the surface of the skin.

2. Enjoy the giving.

If, as the giver/doer, we are not enjoying the experience, our partner will probably sense it and hold back in some way.

We can be aware of our partner's pleasure without forgetting our own. There can be many wonderful sensations on our lips, tongue, and throughout our mouth.

3. One gives, One receives—most of the time.

When we are the active doer, we are less likely to feel the subtle nuances. Invite your lover to lie back and receive, then she or he can reciprocate another time.

Of course, if you both are having fun giving, forget this guideline. Pleasure is more important than theory.

4. Lots of lubrication, with most strokes.

If your mouth is dry, eat a grape, suck on a lemon, or make a sucking sound with your tongue and lower lip in order to "milk" the saliva gland ducts under the tongue.

No No's

HERE ARE SOME MAJOR don'ts—based on much trial and ERROR.

- No vinegar undiluted. The cover of this book is a fantasy only, at least on membranous tissue.
- No sandpaper. Hair stubbles hurt. Check your face, underarms, legs, and pubic area first if you usually shave there.
- No sugared ingredients inside the vagina. Happy yeast = Hot crotch.
- Birth control jellies and foam taste horrible.
- So do many perfumes, scented soaps, oils, and lotions.
- No sucking sounds near the ear. A real mood shifter from hot to cold.

Health

This book is WRITTEN principally from the perspective that neither partner has a communicable condition. Even in the heat of passion, we must, however, remember health concerns. The following suggestions may not apply to everyone but should be taken into consideration.

- Safe-Sex guidelines strongly advocate barrier protection, usually condoms on the penis and latex dental dams on female genitals. (Dental dams, usually used by dentists, are large enough to cover the vaginal opening and thin enough to feel through. Some types of plastic wrap might also be sufficient barrier protectors.)

- Avoid contact with any area with skin infections.
- Never force air into the vagina, which might cause an air embolism.
- There are many sensual, sensitive nerve endings in the anal area, but oral-anal sex is considered very high-risk, unsafe sex behavior without barrier protection.
- This is a basic but incomplete list of health suggestions. It may be wise to consult a physician or health educator for your specific situations.

Oral Aerobics

No pain, no gain is the theme in the gym. Not here. It's fun to build up kissing, sucking, nibbling muscles.

Warm-ups
Here are some serious, semi-serious warm-ups:

- Repeat L words such as *lust, lewd, lascivious*
- Suck a licorice string
- Practice touching your nose with your tongue
- Lick lots of lollipops
- Dial your telephone with your tongue
- Learn to speak French, especially "Oh, la la"
- Curl your tongue and slide it in and out
- Learn to play a trumpet: Try double-tonguing (*TA-CA, TA-CA, TA-CA*) and triple-tonguing (*TA-DE-CA, TA-DE-CA, TA-DE-CA*)
- Suck and tongue the jelly out of a donut

- Put a condom on with your mouth
- Tie cherry stems with your tongue
- Remove your lover's clothes with just your mouth
- Practice deep-throating long-neck bottles
- Or peeled bananas

Tongue Kung Fu

This is an ancient Chinese technique described in *Taoist Secrets of Love* by Mantak Chia.

Hang an orange on a string and practice martial arts with your tongue.

- Jab the orange.
- Lift it up with an upward sliding motion.
- Slap it from side to side.
- After a few weeks graduate to a grapefruit.
- And to prepare for the Olympics, practice with a jar filled with weights.

But Do You Swallow?

To swallow or not to swallow—it's a question often asked. The answer is simple: Only if you want to. In any lovemaking, oral or otherwise, never force yourself. Explore, be open to new experiences, from time to time maybe try something you didn't like in the past. Sexual play is an evolving process.

If you don't like the flavor of your lover's ejaculation, here is a *Sex Shake* formula from Harley SwiftDeer, a shaman of Native American descent.

Sex Shake

2 tsp. honey
1 cup milk
1/4 tsp. ground cinnamon
1/4 tsp. ground ginger
1/4 tsp. ground nutmeg
1/4 tsp. ground cloves
1 raw egg

Blend and drink 1 hour prior to lovemaking

But what about female ejaculation? Yes, at least some women can ejaculate. However, I have not heard of any complaints about the flavor nor any special Sex Shakes to alter the taste.

Fever When You Kiss Me — 1001 Ways

Well, here it's more like eighteen ways. With all the possible combinations and permutations, however, we'll have at least 1001 ways to pleasure our lover.

The sections are divided into whether the emphasis is on the tongue, the lips, the teeth, or the breath.

These oral strokes can be planned or spontaneous. Most of all, let the moods and responses unfold as they may.

Lots of saliva or some other lubricant is essential for many of the following strokes. Consult the "Top Secrets" chapter on a dry day.

The Tongue

Ice Cream Lick

Just like licking a cone of your favorite flavor. This stroke is the best way to lubricate the skin with saliva, which will be necessary for many of the other strokes. To give an Ice Cream Lick, make a gentle, full tongue stroke of one to three inches, each time with lots of saliva. Continue till your lover becomes all creamy.

Snake Tongue

Slither over your lover's body, flitting just the tip of your tongue lightly and rapidly up and down. An especially sensuous feeling if you have already applied saliva.

Tongue Thrust

Slightly stiffen your tongue and thrust it out for its full extended length. Then return it. Be sure to vary the speed and pressure of the thrust—some slow and easy, some fast and hard. A thrill for orifices and between fingers and toes.

The Lips

Lipstick

After applying saliva to your lover's skin, moisten your own lips, thoroughly. Without any suction, gently slide your lips back and forth over the skin.

Succulent Suction

Place the entire edge of your lips on your lover's skin and, creating suction in your mouth, lift up the skin and maybe the muscle beneath. Hold each suction for a couple of seconds and let go with a sumptuous kissing sound.

If your lover wants a hickey, simply intensify the suction. Voilà!

 ## Suck and Slide

First apply a lot of saliva. Create a suction, and while maintaining it and a full lip contact, slide along the path of saliva.

 # Suck, Slide, and Twirl

Start with Suck and Slide and add the magic of a twirling tongue. It is very important to keep the suction here. Don't be surprised if your lover ravishes you after this.

 # Lollipop

Applied to any appendage that fits neatly into your mouth. Just imagine that this appendage is a sweet lollipop and give a Suck, Slide, and Twirl while your partner melts and becomes juicy.

Clitoral Kiss

Quite adaptable to any pleasurable protuberance, such as the earlobe, fingertip, or clitoris.
Focus your lips around the selected flesh. By creating a vacuum in your mouth, suck the small protuberance between your lips into your mouth. Then, while maintaining a gentle suction, squeeze your lips and tongue together so that the protuberance slides outward. Continue without stopping the suction or contact.

Hummin'

Place your lips on or around any part of the body and hum. Make sure the tune fits the mood.

 # Daisy Kisses

Simple, light, cheery kisses, like when falling in love.

 # MOTORBOAT

Pucker your lips together while forcing the breath through them so as to make a motorboat sound. This may sound like kids' stuff until you feel it on your clitoris, navel, or scrotum.

The Teeth

Fairies Dance

Very lightly slide the tips of the front teeth across the skin. Just the teeth, without lips or mustache touching. Depending on the body contours, use either the upper teeth or both the upper and lower. This stroke may feel like tiny fairies dancing across the skin.

Nibbles

Here your teeth give one- or two-second nibbles large enough to include both skin and muscle beneath. Especially nice for larger muscle areas. On the throat, breasts, inner thighs, and genitals, be very delicate.

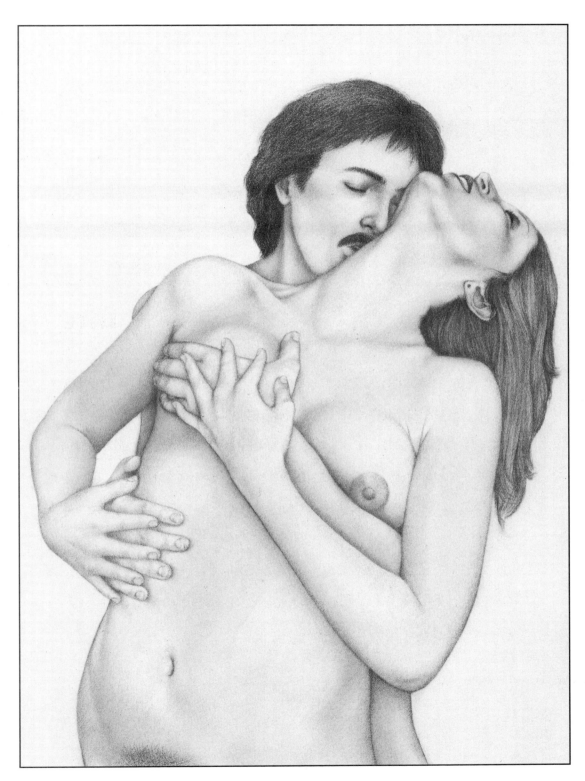

Kyle Spencer

Tiger Love Bite

This must be done with care and sensitivity to keep your partner coming back for more.

Locate a thick and perhaps tight muscle, maybe along the upper shoulder or the back of the neck. Slowly sink your bite into the muscle until you sense the edge of pain, then bite a tiny bit more. Hold for a fleeting moment or, if your lover is moaning with pleasure, for a couple of seconds before releasing.

Slip and Slide

Lubricate the skin well with saliva. Start as if biting but allow the upper and lower rows of teeth to slide toward each other without pinching.

The Breath

Gentle Breezes

Making a small opening between your lips, blow Gentle Breezes from about three to six inches away from your lover's body. Especially cooling after passionate play has brought moisture to the skin's surface.

Sun Kiss

Open your mouth very close to the skin, shape your throat and tongue as if to pronounce the syllable "ha," and without saying a word, breathe a warm glow to your lover's body and soul by exhaling. The Sun Kiss nicely complements Fairies Dance and Lipstick.

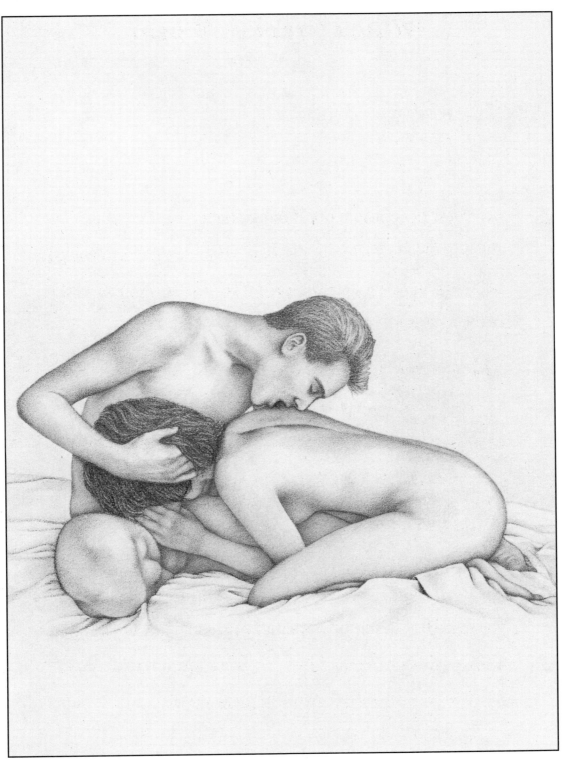

KYLE SPENCER

Which Strokes Where

There is no magic point or technique for any person all the time. What can limit us the most is the assumption that what delighted us in the past will ensure ecstasy again. Stay in the present, attend to subtle nuances.

Thighs: inner and backsides

Focus on upward movements from the knee toward the genital or buttock areas. This is a great place to give a Suck and Slide. A lot of sexual energy lies in the thighs.

Buttocks

Prepare your lover with some sweet Ice Cream Licks and Suck and Slides. After a while when you find a spot where you easily feel muscle beneath the fatty tissue, slowly sink your teeth in with a Tiger Love Bite. Then release. If it is just right, maybe only a minute or two will be bearable.

At the end, be sure to give some Daisy Kisses.

Back of the Neck and Upper Shoulders

I have seen more orgasmic responses result from touch here than from any other part of the body except for the clitoris, G-spot, and penis. My favorite here is the Tiger Love Bite again. It is best introduced when your partner is already in the heat of passion. Always be sensitive on tense, sore muscles.

Breasts

To begin, you might start with a Suck and Slide up the inner arm, across the upper part of the underarm and down to the breast. (Spread lots of saliva first.) Continue this stroke all around the breasts. Sliding to the nipples, intermix the Suck and Slide with the Clitoral Kiss.

Woman's Genitals

Introduce your mouth to her vulva with an Ice Cream Lick between the outer and inner lips as well as between the inner lips. Next, Snake Tongue the inner lips and clitoral area.

After suggesting to your lover that she hold on, Suck and Twirl the clitoris. Now the Clitoral Kiss followed by the Tongue Thrust into the vaginal orifice.

Some enjoyable additions include the Motorboat (you'll have to spread the pubic hair and labia to the sides), Gentle Breezes, and Hummin'.

Man's Genitals

All the following strokes can be pleasurable on either an erect, semi-erect, or flaccid penis:

Ice Cream Lick the whole scrotum and penis until it oozes with saliva. Savor this as if you were licking real homemade peaches and banana ice cream.

Slither around the scrotum with the Snake Tongue. Maybe try Hummin' with his scrotum, half or whole, gently in your mouth. Then play with Gentle Breezes and the Sun Kiss.

On the sides of the shaft start slowly with very moist Lipstick movements. Gradually with more lip contact and suction, you will have a Suck and Slide. Then top it off with the Lollipop, keeping the suction while your tongue engulfs the head. If in his ecstasy your partner forgets to breathe, remind him to inhale.

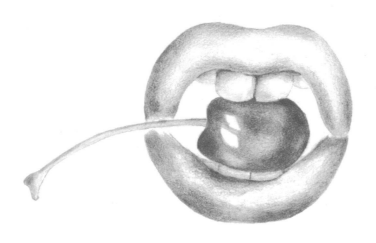

Smother Your Lover in

Chocolate Syrup

and . . .

Smother Your Lover in Chocolate Syrup and . . .

The erotic ritual that follows is only for the adventurous. When you are ready for two or three hours of playful abandonment, welcome to The Garden of Earthly Delights.

Here are some of the preparations.

First select a bed sheet that may never get thoroughly clean afterwards. Maybe have a large sheet of plastic to protect the carpet, bed, or wherever the ritual will be held.

You'll probably need to schedule a shopping trip. Fully ripened fruits may not be available at the market. So it would be best to purchase these a few days before the evening (or afternoon) of earthly delights.

Here is what takes place in The Garden. A variety of fruits, nuts, and sauces are to be prepared. Your lover's nude body, of course, will be the foundation for the exotic sculpture. But this will be living, participatory art. You, in epicurean fashion, partake fully of your creation. Meanwhile, your lover, who just happens to be beneath your tongue, may well be entering the realm of rapture.

KYLE SPENCER

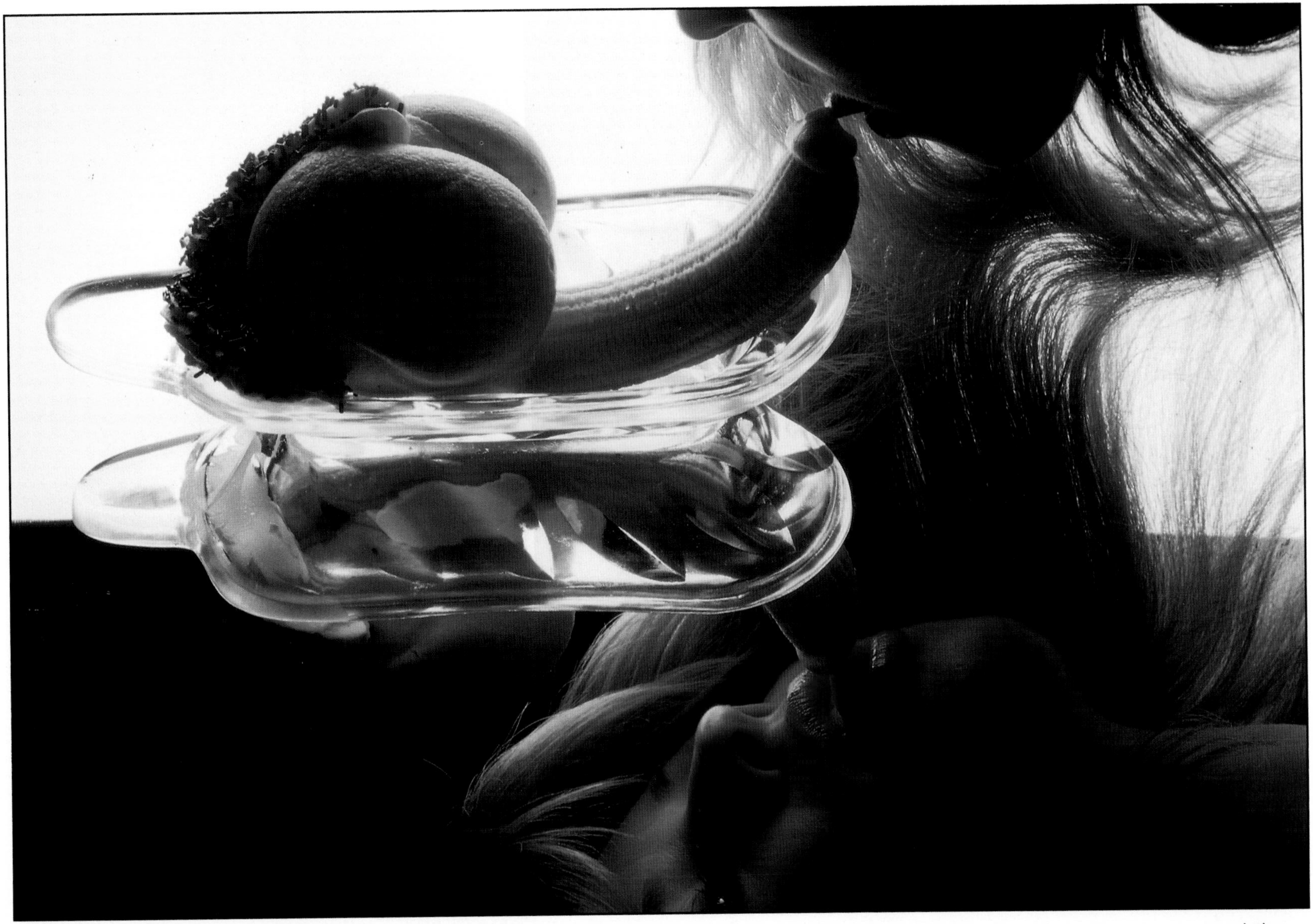

David Thorpe

Richard Stodar

Kyle Spencer

11

KYLE SPENCER

Rick van Genderen

Here are a few fresh fruit suggestions.

The Goddess must have been defining the essence of pleasure when she created the mango. Golden in color with the sweetness of heavenly nectar and the texture of sexual satisfaction, this fruit delights both the palate of the feaster and the one feasted upon.

Other sumptuous choices would be papaya, bananas, strawberries, cherries, kiwi, seedless grapes, and maybe persimmons. One or two varieties of melons would make The Garden even juicier. Citrus fruits may not blend well with the following chocolate and cream sauces. Let your desire be your guide.

For the nuts, good possibilities are almonds, walnuts, and pecans. Some of these could be roasted but not heavily salted.

A selection of sauces will make the feast even more luscious. Chocolate syrup is one. And if you have never tried real maple syrup, the darker grades are heavenly.

For many connoisseurs, slightly sweetened, hand-whipped

whipped cream is a must. To make it almost orgasmic, purchase the thickest cream possible.

For faster whipped cream, purchase the kind in pressurized cans and apply on your lover with flamboyant flair.

For another special sauce, mix heated honey or maple syrup with sour cream or plain yogurt. Sweeten to the flavor that fits your tastes.

(Remember, sugar in the vagina means lots of Happy Yeast.)

After all the selections are gathered, you'll need about two hours of preparation before the actual ritual. Also, since you create your sculpture directly on your lover's skin, minimize chilled substances. Keep all fruits at room temperature and warm the sauces that are heatable.

As the appointed hour approaches, begin to fashion an erotic ambiance. Make sure the room is warm. Unplug the phone, light candles, and select music. Do anything necessary to create a sense that there will be no interruptions.

When all is prepared, escort your beloved into the ceremonial chamber. After assisting with the disrobing, invite him or her to recline beside the beautifully prepared platters and bowls.

In a soft voice, ask your lover to let you know if any sensation or experience becomes undesirable. Otherwise, the only permissible vocal expressions will be moans and groans. Suggest taking a deep breath and allowing the eyes to close.

Then, turn the music up a little, cease verbal chatter, and enter The Garden of Earthly Delights.

Just smother your lover in chocolate syrup and boogie till the cows come home.

It Ain't Fattening

But It May Be Illegal

In stark contrast to this view of a natural, loving expression, there is a disheartening fact: oral-genital contact between consenting adults is illegal in twenty-three states, the District of Columbia, and all branches of the U.S. Military.

Alabama
Arizona
Arkansas
Florida
Georgia
Idaho
Kansas
Louisiana
Maryland
Massachusetts
Minnesota
Mississippi
Missouri
Montana
Nevada
North Carolina

Oklahoma
Rhode Island
South Carolina
Tennessee
Texas
Utah
Virginia

District of Columbia

U.S. Air Force
U.S. Army
U.S. Coast Guard
U.S. Marines
U.S. Navy

Such oppressive, puritanical laws are contrary to the fundamental functioning of a free society.

I strongly encourage you to join and financially support, as I do, organizations and political candidates who are dedicated to the freedom of choice, who truly understand the meaning of "life, liberty, and the pursuit of happiness."

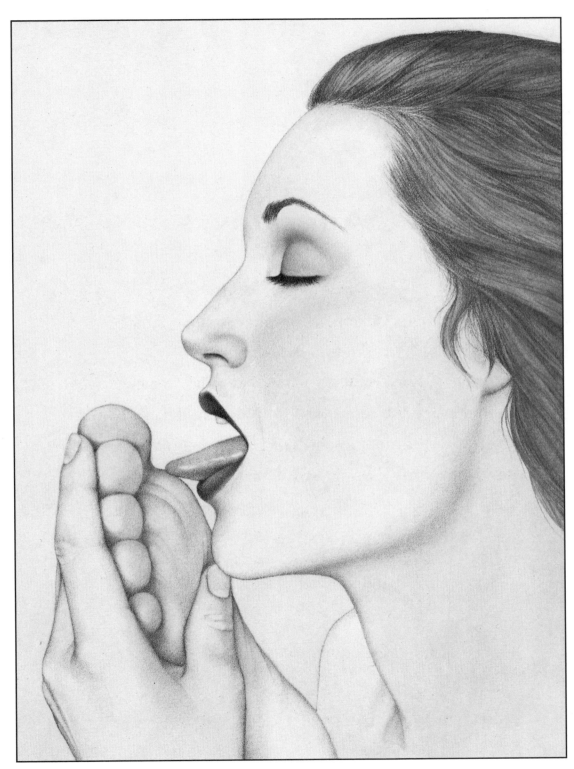

Kyle Spencer

Appendix:

ANCIENT LOVE MANUALS

Richard Stodart

ANCIENT LOVE MANUALS

Lovers throughout the centuries have sought new ways to pleasure one another. "Pillow books" of many different sorts have appeared to fulfill such inquiries.

These manuals generally were for the educated upper classes and royalty. Reading the translations, we often find worlds that today seem exotic, erotic, and sometimes esoteric. Unfortunately these texts sometimes reflect rather sexist, provincial views of the author and the culture.

In the following selections, I have usually eliminated the gender-specific language. Still, some of the techniques might seem bizarre or intense, maybe boring at times.

Biblical Cunnilingus

Granted *The Bible* is not much of a sex manual, but the founding patriarchy let one slip through in *The Song of Songs*.

> My beloved is gone down into his garden, to the beds of spices,
>   to feed in the gardens, and to gather lilies.
> I am my beloved's, and my beloved is mine; he feedeth among the lilies.

The Kama Sutra

Approximately 2,000 years ago, a Hindu sage, Vatsyayana, sat down to write what was to become the Western world's most well-known love manual. This was a time and a location where sexuality and pleasure were practically devoid of sin and religious guilt.

The Kama Sutra is neither pornographic nor erotic. Many find reading the whole text laborious. The book really is more a treatise on appropriate social behavior. Almost all of the Kama Sutra oral techniques are included here.

Kama Sutra Kisses

- *Nominal Kiss*

    When our lips touch our beloved's but do nothing else.

- *Throbbing Kiss*

    When our lower lip moves our lover's lower lip but not the upper.

- *Touching Kiss*

    When our tongue touches our lover's lip and, closing our eyes, our hands touch our beloved's.

- *Straight Kiss*

    When we bring our lips into direct contact with our lover's lips.

- *Bent Kiss*

    When lovers bend their heads toward each other and kiss.

- *Turned Kiss*

    When we hold our beloved's hand and chin and turn the face upward to kiss.

- *Pressed Kiss*

    When we press our lover's lower lip with much force.

- *Greatly Pressed Kiss*

    When we take hold of our lover's lip with two fingers, and then after touching it with our tongue, we press the lip with great force using our lips.

- *Kiss of the Upper Lip*

    When we kiss our lover's upper lip while our partner in return kisses our lower lip.

- *A Clasping Kiss*

    When we take both of our lover's lips between our own.

- *Fighting of the Tongue*

    When during "A Clasping Kiss" our beloved's tongue touches our teeth, tongue, and the palate.

- *Kiss that Kindles Love*

    When we look at the face of our beloved asleep and kiss the face to show our intention or desire.

- *Kiss that Turns Away*

    When we kiss in order to turn our lover's attention away from business, quarreling, or looking at something else.

- *Kiss that Awakens*

    When arriving home late at night, we kiss our beloved who is asleep in order to show our desire.

- *Kiss Showing the Intention*

    When we kiss the reflection of our beloved in the mirror, in water, or on a wall.

- *Demonstrative Kiss*

    When, if our lover is standing, we kiss our lover's finger, or if sitting, we kiss our lover's thigh or great toe.

KAMA SUTRA BITING

- *Hidden Bite*

    When the biting is shown only by the excessive redness of the skin that is bitten.

- *Swollen Bite*

    When the skin is pressed down on both sides.

- *The Point*

    When a small portion of the skin is bitten with two teeth only.

- *The Line of Points*

    When small portions of the skin are bitten with all the teeth.

- *Coral and the Jewel*

    When biting is done by bringing together the teeth and the lips.

- *The Line of Jewels*

    When biting is done with all the teeth.

- *The Broken Cloud*

  When biting results in unequal risings in a circle and comes from the space between the teeth.
- *The Biting of a Boar*

  When biting consists of many broad rows of marks near to one another resulting in red internals.

Kama Sutra "Mouth Congress"

This is on the male genitals only. Sorry, but the *Kama Sutra* doesn't describe clitoral kissing.

- *Nominal Congress*

  When holding our lover's lingam (penis) in our hand, we place our lips around the lingam and move our mouth all about.
- *Biting the Sides*

  When we press the sides of our lover's lingam with our lips and teeth.
- *Outside Pressing*

  When we press the end of the lingam with our lips close together and kiss it with suction as if we were drawing it out.
- *Inside Pressing*

  When we place our lover's lingam into our mouth and pressing with our lips, we slide it out.
- *Kissing*

  When we kiss the lingam as if we were kissing the lower lip.
- *Rubbing*

  When we stroke our lover's lingam all over with our tongue.
- *Sucking a Mango Fruit*

  When we place half of our lover's lingam into our mouth and forcibly kiss and suck it.
- *Swallowing It Up (Deep Throat 2000 years ago)*

  When we place the whole lingam into our mouth and press it to the very end, as if we were going to swallow it up.

The Ananga-Ranga

About fourteen centuries after the *Kama Sutra*, the *Ananga-Ranga* appears, likewise from India though after Muslim invasions. The oral lovemaking practices are somewhat similar.

Both books were translated into English in the late 1800's for an eager British audience. Due to censorship, however, these two love manuals were not to be made extensively available to the general public until the 1960's.

Ananga-Ranga Kissing

- *Reconciling Kissing*

    When our lover is angry, we, forcibly, fix our lips upon our beloved's and continue with both mouths united till the ill-temper ceases.

- *Sphurita-Kissing*

    Here we bring our mouth to our lover's who then kisses our lower lip whilst we draw away in a jerking manner without any return of a kiss.

- *Neck-Nape Kissing*

    After covering and closing our lover's eyes with our hands, and closing our own eyes, we thrust our tongue into our lover's mouth and move it to and fro with a motion so pleasant and slow that it at once suggests another form of enjoyment.

- *Oblique Kissing*

    Standing beside or behind our lover, we lift our lover's chin toward the sky; then we take our beloved's lower lip between our teeth, gently biting and chewing.

- *Upper-Lip Kissing*

    While we gently bite and chew our lover's lower lip, our partner reciprocates on our upper lip to the heights of passion.

- *Lump-Kissing*
    We hold our lover's lips with our fingers, pass our tongue over them and bite them.
- *Casket-Kissing*
    When our lover kisses the inside of our mouth while we do the same.
- *Hanuvatra-Kissing*
    While advancing our lips towards one another, hesitating, and frolicking, we finally kiss.
- *Awakening Kiss*
    When upon finding our lover sleeping, we fix our lips upon our lover's, gradually increasing the pressure until sleep becomes desire.
- *Samaushtha Kissing*
    When we take the mouth and lips of our beloved's, press with our tongue, and dance about.

Ananga-Ranga Biting
- *Secret Biting*
    When we apply our teeth only to the inner or red part of our lover's lip, leaving no outside marks so as to remain unseen by the world.
- *Uchun-Dashana*
    When we bite any part of our beloved's lips or cheeks.
- *Coral Biting*
    When there is a "wonderful union" between our teeth and our beloved's lips.
- *Drop-Biting*
    When we leave the mark of our two front teeth upon our lover's lower lip or brow.
- *A Rosary*
    Same as the preceding drop-biting except all the front teeth are applied.

- *Khandabhrak*

  When our teeth leave a cluster of impressions upon our beloved's brow, cheek, neck, and breast.

- *Kolacharcha*

  When in the heat of passion we leave deep and lasting marks of our teeth upon our beloved's body.

Chinese Wisdom

Many of the sexual practices in Chinese literature come to us from medical and meditation texts. Much of the description is poetic with alluring imagery, a refreshing contrast to the often vulgar tone in English-language depictions.

Rather than using full translations of the original texts, here I draw from two contemporary books far more accessible: *The Tao of Sexology* by Dr. Stephen T. Chang and *The Tao of Love and Sex* by Jolan Chang.

- The latter book recommends two ways to improve erotic kissing. First, relax the oral and facial muscles. Second, pay close attention to the sense of touch, smell, taste, and sound. Unpleasant odors after eating, smoking, or drinking can distract.

- *The Tao of Sexology* suggests erotic kissing as foreplay on the female body. While touching in various places with our hands, we begin kissing, licking, and breathing on and around our lover's stomach acupuncture meridian beginning near the eye and forehead, flowing down to the nipple and on down to the pelvis near the genitals. Now starting on the bottom of the foot, we continue the kissing, licking, and breathing up the kidney meridian on the leg to the genitals.

  If done sufficiently, our lover "can be brought up to the fourth level of orgasm."